# Cathy Bellows

# FOUR FAT RATS

## Macmillan Publishing Company
### New York

Collier Macmillan Publishers
London

For Charles

Macmillan Publishing Company
866 Third Avenue, New York, NY 10022
Collier Macmillan Canada, Inc.
Printed and bound by South China Printing Company, Hong Kong
First American Edition

10 9 8 7 6 5 4 3 2

The text of this book is set in 16 point Horley Old Style.
The illustrations are rendered in watercolor.
Library of Congress Cataloging-in-Publication Data
Bellows, Cathy. Four fat rats.
Summary: Four fat sassy rats leave home and eat a wide swathe
through the world, alienating everybody on the way.
[1. Rats—Fiction.   2. Greed—Fiction]   I. Title.   II. Title: 4 fat rats.
PZ7.B4195Fo   1987   [E]   85-31836
ISBN 0-02-708830-8

$M$r. Rat was very big.

Mrs. Rat was rather large.

And when they had babies, they didn't have ordinary babies.

Oh, no! They had great big fat rat babies. Four fat rats, to be exact.

Mama and Papa were very, very proud.

Every day the four fat rats grew bigger and fatter
and rattier and rattier, till one day Mama and Papa
decided it was time to send them out into the wide world.

"Now, as soon as you get into the wide world," said Papa, "you must gather some leaves and twigs till you have a nice cozy nest, just right for a rat."

"And remember, my darlings," said Mama, "you are rats! You must be bold and sassy and as ratty as possible. Nothing less will do."

Then she gave them each a bite on the nose, and Papa gave them each a bite on the nose, and out into the wide world the four rats waddled.

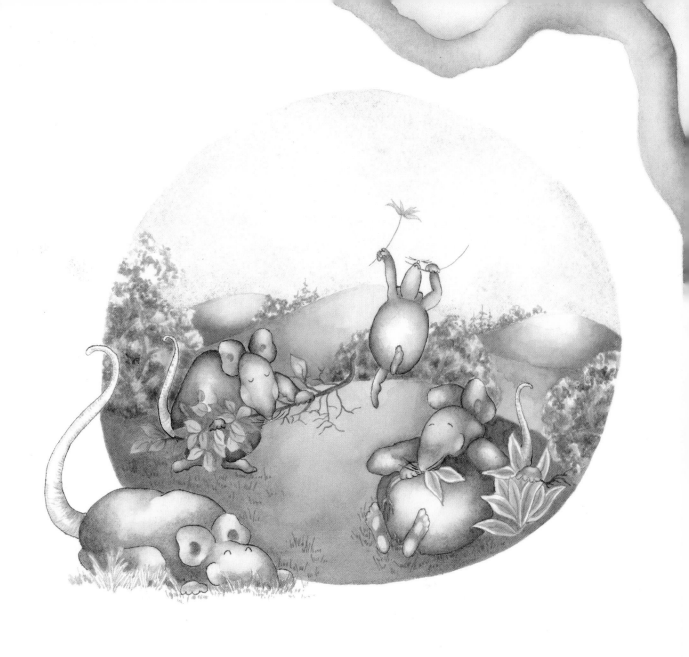

Oh, what a place the wide world was! It was simply delicious. There were leaves to munch on and twigs to crunch on. There were flowers to gobble and grasses to gulp, and though the fat rats wanted to build a nest, they just couldn't find the time. They were too busy eating.

Finally nighttime came, and the four fat rats began to shiver with cold. But they weren't the least bit worried, for they were fat and they were rats and they were sure there was someone around who would take them in. So they waddled into the deep dark forest to look for a place to sleep.

Now, in the deep dark forest, not far from the rats, there happened to be a rabbit hole tucked into the hollow of a tree. It was a very cozy rabbit hole, with a door and a window, and when the four rats saw it, they thought it was perfect, just right for a rat!

So they knocked at the door and looked in the window. "Hello," they said. "Anybody home? Rats are here!"

Rats?! Deep inside the rabbit hole, Mr. and Mrs. Rabbit were getting ready for bed. "Rats?!" they whispered. "Could there really be rats outside our door?" They crept down the hallway and peeked outside.

Sure enough, there they were: four huge, gigantic rats, with beady eyes and sharp teeth and long pointy tails. The poor rabbits almost fainted with fright.

"Hurry, my fluffy ones," cried Mr. Rabbit. "We've got to get out of here." And out the back window they hopped.

Meanwhile, the four fat rats stood outside, knocking and yelling and making a terrible racket, until finally they just opened the door and let themselves in.

"Mmm," sighed the first rat, taking a bite out of the rabbits' table. "What a delicious place this is."

"So tastefully decorated," said the second, munching on a chair.

"Just right for a rat!" said the third, jumping in the bed.

"I think we should stay!" declared the fourth.

And they would have stayed, too. But the next morning when they awoke, they noticed that right above them, at the top of a tree, there lived a whole village of squirrels. The squirrels had very nice nests and crunchy crackly nuts to eat, and best of all, they were high in the sky—what a view!

It drove the fat rats crazy!—especially the view.

"Just look at those squirrels up there!" cried the fourth rat. "It's a disgrace the way they're always looking down on us."

"There they are way up there, and here we are way down here," said the third. "Why, it doesn't seem right. Us rats should be on top!"

"And so we shall be!" said the second rat, and being very ratty and very sassy, he climbed right up that tree. *"Ugkkk! Oompf!"* It wasn't easy for a fat rat to climb, but he did it anyway, and when he reached the top the other three followed.

Yes, home in the treetops was just right for a rat. The four fat rats had a wonderful view, they could look down on everybody, and whenever they got hungry, they just stepped onto a limb, and—*klonk!*—the squirrels provided them with all the nuts they could eat.

But one day the rats happened to catch sight of a barn in the distance, with cows standing outside the door.

"Why, look at that!" said the first rat. "Look at the house those cows live in. It's huge!"

"I think it's a barn," said the second rat.

"Of course it's a barn," said the first rat, "but it's a painted barn, and look, it even has a fence to keep the riffraff out."

"A fence!" cried the third rat. "Why, the very idea. Here we are, living in an old tree with squirrels running all over the place, and there they are, living in a barn with a fence."

"If anyone's going to live in a barn," said the fourth rat, "I think it ought to be us rats."

So out of the tree they climbed, and across the fields they marched.

"Oh, my," said the Guernsey cow. "Don't look now, girls, but I see four great big fat rats, and they're headed this way."

"Just ignore them," said the Jersey nearby. "Just pay no attention to them and they'll go away."

The rats didn't go away. They marched right past the cows. "Hello, ladies," they said, and marched on toward the barn.

"Look!" bellowed the Guernsey. "They're headed right into our barn."

"Don't worry," said the Jersey. "Remember the bull. If they go inside the barn, the bull will take care of them."

Sure enough, as soon as the rats stepped inside the
barn, the bull began to stomp and snarl and snort
something awful. "Out of my barn!" he bellowed.

But the rats paid no attention. After all, the great
big bull was tied in his stall, and the four fat rats had
the run of the place.

What a life! The four fat rats ate the very best
kernels off the very best corn cobs. They took their
baths in the cows' drinking water, and they made their
beds in the horses' oats. They tiptoed all through the
chicken feed and played catch in the pigs' slop.
Nobody could stand them—not the cows, not the
horses, not the chickens, not even the pigs. But the
rats didn't care. After all, they were rats and they were
fat, and every day they got bigger and fatter and rattier
and sassier.

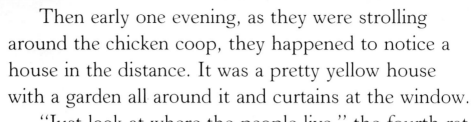

Then early one evening, as they were strolling around the chicken coop, they happened to notice a house in the distance. It was a pretty yellow house with a garden all around it and curtains at the window.

"Just look at where the people live," the fourth rat cried, pointing to the house. "They live in a house, a yellow house!"

"So what?" said the first rat. "Who cares? Our barn is much bigger and it's painted red."

"Bigger, yes," said the fourth rat. "But does it have a garden all around it? No…we've got a pigsty around our house. And do we have curtains at the windows? No…we don't even have windows!"

And when they looked at their barn, they saw it was true. *Yuk!* So over to the house they waddled, to get a closer look.

Inside the window they peeked. They saw rugs on the floor and pictures on the wall and a big bag of garbage under the sink. But that wasn't all.

"Just look at those people," whispered the fourth rat. "Look! They're wearing clothes!"

"Clothes!" cried the third rat. "And here we are, naked in our fur!"

"It's a disgrace!" said the second rat. "That's what it is, a disgrace. Us rats have to live in a barn with animals, while those people sit in their fine house. Why, they don't even have tails."

It was too much for the fat rats. So they waited till dark, till the farmer and his wife went to sleep. Then into that yellow house they crept.

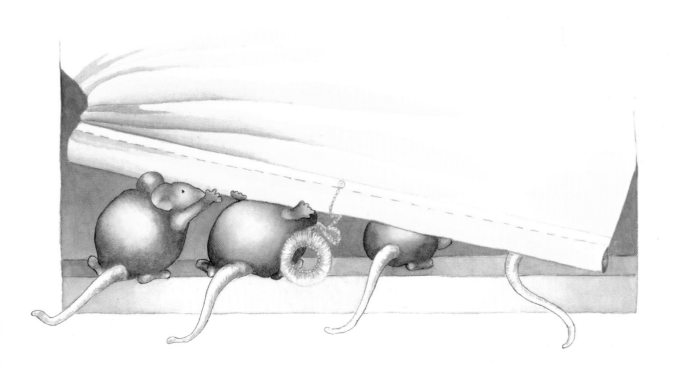

One, two, three, four—oh, they were sneaky rats.
Four, three, two, one—under the rug they crawled.
Carefully they turned on the light, cautiously they
opened up a sewing box, and then ever so quietly they
began to dress for dinner.

Ribbons, buttons, beads—nothing was too fine for
the rats. They draped lace round their shoulders and
hung safety pins from their ears, and when they were
perfectly perfect, they took each other by the arm and
into the kitchen they pranced.

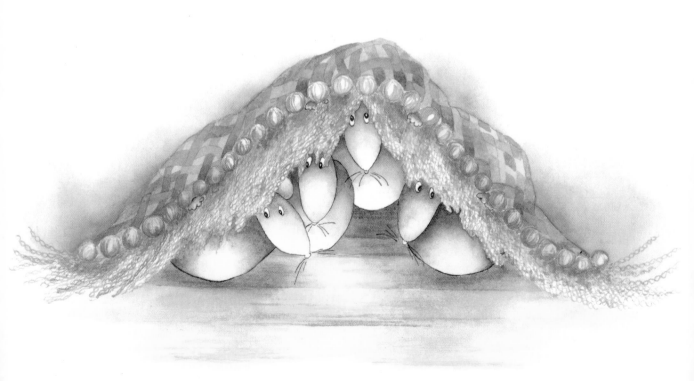

First stop was the garbage bag. They ate eggshells and teabags and coffee grinds galore. They nibbled on orange peels, banana peels, potato peels, and onion peels. They devoured crumbs and noodles and pieces of fat. And when they were stuffed, when they were so stuffed they could barely fit another crumb between their little ratty lips, that's when they noticed the pie.

It was a blueberry pie, a big juicy pie that sat on the kitchen table and shimmered in the morning light. Who could resist? Not the four fat rats! They gobbled that pie right down.

"Oh, my," sighed the first rat as she sat on the edge of the pie plate, licking her paws. "You know, I just can't believe how clever we are."

"And how rich we are," said the second, wiping his whiskers.

"And how lovely we are," said the third.

"And how fat we are," said the fourth.

And fat they were. For when they tried to get up—*Ugkkk!*—they found they were too fat to move.

They could hear the people stirring upstairs. What a panic! "We've got to get out of here!" they cried, but it was no use.

They tried rolling onto their feet, they tried crawling down the table, they tried pushing themselves up with their tails, but try as they might, they couldn't budge.

*Clomp! Clomp! Clomp!* Down the stairs came the people.

*Stomp! Stomp! Stomp!* Into the kitchen they marched.

"Rats!" screamed the little old lady.

"Rats!" yelled the little old man.

"Oh, rats," said the fat rats, and before they knew what was happening, *swoosh!* Across the kitchen the four rats flew.

*Whoompf!* Out the door they tumbled. Round and round they rolled, past the cows' barn, with the cows all laughing.

On and on they rolled, under the squirrels' tree, with the squirrels all screeching.

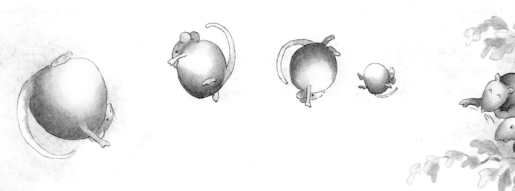

Farther and farther they rolled, over the rabbits' hole, with the rabbits all giggling.

They rolled and they rolled, till finally they rolled right past their old rats' nest.

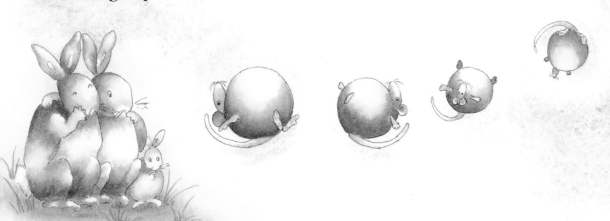

"Papa! Papa!" cried their mama, as the rats went rolling by. "Just look at our babies! Oh, Papa, aren't they darling? Aren't they adorable?"

"Aren't they fat?"

And they were, too.

They were very fat.

They were the four fat rats.